TWO WE[...]   THE PLAY

Mary Morris has been writing since [...] roductions of her
plays include several for young audiences. She also writes for
mainstream theatre and for television. *Two Weeks with the Queen*
is Mary's second adaptation. In 1990 she adapted Robin Klein's
nov[...]   *ith the Queen* and *Boss of
the P[...]* have [...] tours in Australia.

Born in the UK, Morris Gleitzman moved to Australia with his
family at the age of sixteen. His career took off as a screenwriter
and a newspaper columnist, before he became a successful
author. He has written a number of children's books including
Two Weeks with the Queen, *Misery Guts*, *Worry Warts*, *Blabber
Mouth* (the first Rowena Batts story), and *Sticky Beak*. He now
lives in Melbourne and has two children.

Reviews

TWO WEEKS WITH THE QUEEN

'A gem of a book' *Guardian*

'A remarkably exciting, moving and funny book' *Children's
Books of the Year*

'One of the best books I've ever read. I wish I'd written it!'
Paula Danziger

MISERY GUTS

'Totally compelling.' *Children's Books of the Year*

BLABBER MOUTH

'Gleitzman tells his story brilliantly and with enormous
humour.' Julia Eccleshare, *The Bookseller*

TWO WEEKS WITH THE QUEEN

THE PLAY

MARY MORRIS

Adapted from the novel by

MORRIS GLEITZMAN

MACMILLAN
CHILDREN'S BOOKS

First published 1993 by Currency Press Ltd

This edition published 1994 by Macmillan Children's Books
a division of Macmillan Publishers Limited
20 New Wharf Road, London N1 9RR
Basingstoke and Oxford
www.panmacmillan.com

Associated companies throughout the world

ISBN 0-330-33693-2

7 9 10 8

A CIP catalogue record for this book is available from
the British Library

Phototypeset by Intype, London
Printed and bound in Great Britain by
Mackays of Chatham PLC, Chatham, Kent

Characters

COLIN MUDFORD	a twelve-year-old boy
LUKE	Colin's younger brother
MUM	
DAD	
AUNTIE IRIS	Colin's aunt in England
UNCLE BOB	Colin's uncle in England
ALISTAIR	Colin's cousin in England
GRIFF	an AIDS patient in hospital
TED	Griff's partner

The play is usually by six actors using character doubling for the extra roles.

BUSINESSMAN	NURSE
GUARD	MATRON
AMERICAN TOURIST	FLIGHT ATTENDANT
SPANISH TOURIST	CAPTAIN
PATIENT	POLICEMAN
AIRPORT CHECK-IN STAFF	ENGLISH NURSE
CAFE STAFF	ENGLISH DOCTOR
DOCTOR 1	ENGLISH STUDENT DOCTORS
DOCTOR 2	DR GRAHAM

Setting

The Mudfords' home; hospital in Australia and London; the home of Colin's relations in London; outside Buckingham Palace; on a plane and at the airport in Sydney and London.

The music of God Save the Queen *is heard, followed by the plummy voice of Her Majesty delivering her Christmas message.*

At the Mudfords' place Mum and Dad, barefoot and dressed in shorts, singlets and paper hats, are fanning themselves with a bit torn off a beer carton. They are watching the Queen's Christmas message on TV. Colin, also in shorts and very scuffed brown elastic-sided boots, sits some way from them glaring at an open shoe box containing a pair of sensible black school shoes. His kid brother Luke runs in and out strafing everybody and everything with his new MiG fighter plane. Colin picks up a shoe and looks at it with distaste.

QUEEN: And a very merry Christmas to you all.

COLIN: Merry flamin' Christmas. [*Luke strafes him*] Gerroff!

LUKE: Wanna go?

COLIN: Get lost.

    Luke does a circle of the room shooting down the enemy and swoops on Colin again. Colin throws a shoe at him.

LUKE: He hit me! Dad, he hit me!

DAD: Don't hit your brother, Colin.

COLIN: I didn't . . .

MUM: You heard your father.

COLIN: It was him, he started . . .

1

DAD: That's enough! We're trying to listen to the Queen here.

COLIN: Nobody ever listens to me.

LUKE: That's cos you're not the Queen.

DAD: Just keep it down to a roar, eh?

Dad snuggles Mum closer to him and they settle back with the Queen who rabbits on about equality and justice for all.

COLIN: [*quietly, in Luke's direction*] Lucky for you I'm not the Queen. If I was I'd have you locked in the tower and torture you and put you on the rack till your bones creak and then I'd have your fingernails pulled out one by one and then I'd pour boiling oil on you and hang you from the battlements and then I'd . . .

LUKE: Mum, I don't feel well.

COLIN: Then I'd have you cut open right down the middle and your guts would hang out and all the blow flies would come and the crows would peck out your eyes . . .

LUKE: [*louder*] Mum, I feel sick.

MUM: Serves you right for having four serves of chrissie pud.

COLIN: Four?! I only got three!

LUKE: I do, but. [*He goes back to playing with his MiG.*]

2

COLIN: Prob'ly a strain of heat resistant bacteria in the chrissie pud. If I'd got a *microscope* for Christmas instead of a pair of school shoes I could have run some tests and spotted it. We'll prob'ly all come down with it now.

DAD: Colin, go and shut the back door mate – keep some of the heat out.

COLIN: Why can't he go?

DAD: Cos I asked you to.

COLIN: Yeh, well he'd be quicker, he's got turbo thrusters, I've only got lace-ups.

Mum and Dad exchange a guilty glance.

MUM: Luke, go and shut the door. [*Luke goes, Dad turns the Queen off.*] Love, about the microscope . . .

DAD: Next time, eh?

MUM: We just couldn't stretch to it.

COLIN: I know, the recession.

MUM: Besides, you needed shoes.

COLIN: [*looking at his appalling boots*] No I didn't.

DAD: [*picking up a shoe*] They're pretty snazzy shoes. Bloke could end up Prime Minister in shoes like those.

MUM: They are the ones you liked in the shop – aren't they?

3

COLIN: Yes, they're, um, they're good.

MUM: Colin love, is there something else bothering you?

COLIN: [*shrugging*] Nuh.

DAD: You can talk to us mate, you know that.

COLIN: Well . . .

MUM: Yes love?

COLIN: It's just that . . . well . . .

DAD: Yes?

COLIN: Nobody ever . . .

LUKE: [*entering the room*] Mum. Mum!

As they turn towards Luke, he collapses on the floor. Mum and Dad rush towards him.

COLIN: Pays any attention to me.

The sound of an ambulance is heard.

At the hospital Mum and Dad are waiting anxiously for news. Colin is fidgeting. There is a table nearby, laden with medical bits and pieces including a microscope.

COLIN: Why wouldn't the ambulance driver let me in the ambulance? Eh? I never been in an ambulance. Why wouldn't she?

MUM: [*absently*] Mmmmmm?

4

COLIN: Not as if there wasn't any room.

DAD: Just leave it, son.

COLIN: No Christmas spirit, I reckon.

A doctor enters.

DOCTOR ONE: Mr and Mrs Mudford?

MUM AND DAD: How is he? Is he alright?

DOCTOR ONE: Don't worry, it doesn't look too serious, probably just the excitement of the season.

COLIN: [*to doctor*] I reckon it's gastric.

DOCTOR ONE: Gastric, eh?

COLIN: If it's any help I can tell you what he's eaten today: One bowl of Coco-pops; three jelly snakes; some Licorice Allsorts; a packet of Minties; six gherkins; half a giant pack of Twisties and five chocolate Santas. Then for lunch . . .

DOCTOR ONE: Enough already!

COLIN: You can faint from overeating, I've done it with jelly snakes. You see, the large intestine blocks the flow of blood to the brain . . .

DOCTOR ONE: Thanks for the tip.

COLIN: Maybe an enema would help, or a very large dose of castor oil . . . [*Dad grabs Colin and under the guise of putting an arm round him, clamps his mouth.*]

MUM: You're sure it's nothing serious?

DOCTOR ONE: We've taken a few blood tests and sent them off to Sydney, results will be back in a couple of days. We'll know more then.

MUM: A couple of days!

DAD: There's no way of doing them sooner?

DOCTOR ONE: The top people don't live out here, unfortunately.

MUM: But you said it wasn't serious.

DOCTOR ONE: It's just a precaution. I'm sure you'll have him home again in a couple of days.

DAD: The Doc knows what he's talking about, love. Couple of days and he'll be falling out of trees with the best of them.

MUM: Ray! [*Not in front of the doctor!*]

DAD: Alright, um. . . . .Catching snakes with the best of them?

Mum rolls her eyes.

COLIN: Playing cricket.

DAD: Yes, that's it. Playing cricket. [*He winks at Colin.*]

DOCTOR ONE: I'm sure you're right. If you'd like to pop into the office, we'll get a few details.

MUM: [*to Colin*] You wait here love. We won't be long.

COLIN: But I could have important medical
     information. . . .

DAD: Stay!

*Colin stays. The others leave. He discovers the micro-
scope then goes out and returns pushing the trolley
upon which Luke lies.*

LUKE: Put me back, I'll tell Mum, put me back.

COLIN: Here, give us your arm.

LUKE: What for?

COLIN: I told ya. I just want a little bit of blood to put
     under the microscope.

LUKE: No.

COLIN: Come on, it won't hurt. [*He takes out his Swiss
     army knife.*]

LUKE: Help! Mum! Dad! Help!

COLIN: Shut up willya. Look, if you could see how
     worried they are having to wait for Sydney to do
     the tests. Just give me a little bit of blood, I can check
     it out for germs and put their minds at rest.

LUKE: I don't want to.

COLIN: How could you be so selfish – at Christmas too?

LUKE: Don't care.

COLIN: But it's for Mum and Dad.

7

LUKE: I gave them place mats.

COLIN: Okay. Forget it.

LUKE: Put me back now?

COLIN: Yeh, alright. Hey, I just had an idea. You know when you fell in the creek and scraped your elbow on the old ute chassis that was in there?

LUKE: Yeh.

COLIN: You could have got metal poisoning.

LUKE: But it's nearly better.

COLIN: Yeh, but infection could have got in. Better let me have a look at the scab.

LUKE: You reckon?

Luke twists the elbow to look. Colin looks too. He suddenly picks the scab off.

LUKE: OW! What you do that for!

COLIN: I told you, I just want to check for wriggly things.

Colin dabs at the elbow with a hanky and gets to work at the microscope.

LUKE: I'm gunna tell on you.

COLIN: At school we looked in this dead frog through the microscope and there was all these wriggly things and Mr Blair our biology teacher reckoned they were germs.

LUKE: That was my best scab.

COLIN: [*still looking*] Hey there aren't any. You're a faker. There's nuthin' wrong with you. Not a single germ.

LUKE: Are you sure?

COLIN: Not a single wriggle.

LUKE: Maybe people's blood doesn't wriggle like frogs'.

COLIN: It's not the blood that wriggles, it's the germs. Your blood is as healthy as mine.

LUKE: How do you know? You haven't tested yours.

COLIN: I just know.

LUKE: You have to test it otherwise it's not scientific.

COLIN: Alright, alright. [*He takes out his knife and with great trepidation prepares to cut himself.*]

LUKE: No! Not with that. I got a safety pin in my underdaks. [*He fumbles under the covers.*] Here.

Colin pricks himself with the pin and puts a spot of blood on the hanky. He puts it under the microscope.

Well?

COLIN: Oh no!

LUKE: What?

COLIN: Wriggly things. Omigod. I've got it.

LUKE: Got what?

COLIN: I dunno do I? Something worse than you've got. I'm gonna die. Get me a doctor quick.

LUKE: Doctor nothin'. If they find out what we're doin' you'll get killed anyway. Put me back.

A Nurse arrives and sees Luke.

NURSE: You been to X-Ray and back already, love? I don't know what's up with these orderlies leaving you out here. Too much of a hurry to get their Christmas pud inside them eh?

Colin groans, but the Nurse ignores him and takes Luke back to the ward. Colin staggers about moaning. A doctor enters wearing a red plastic nose and a party hat. He is jingling his car keys and singing a Christmas song.

COLIN: 'Scuse me. You a doctor?

DOCTOR 2: Sort of. But I'm finished for the day. Roast turkey, here I come. [*Colin groans*] You okay mate?

COLIN: I reckon I got gastric. Or worse.

DOCTOR 2: You reckon?

COLIN: Yep. I just tested my blood. Maybe you could give me a second opinion.

DOCTOR 2: Sure. Let's have a look. Hold these a minute.

10

The doctor looks at the hanky through the microscope. Colin checks out the car keys. They have a Mercedes symbol attached. Colin is impressed.

Um, has this hanky been in contact with a dead animal by any chance?

COLIN: Only a frog. I wrapped the frog in it after biology when I took it home in my lunch box.

DOCTOR 2: Sorry I asked.

COLIN: Can you see the germs?

DOCTOR 2: Yep. But they're not yours, they're the frog's. You, by the look of you, are as fit as a bullock.

COLIN: Well, how come when I put my brother's blood under there on the same hanky there was no germs?

DOCTOR 2: That bit of the hanky must have stayed clean, by some miracle.

COLIN: [*disappointed*] You mean I'm not gonna die?

DOCTOR 2: Not for a bit. Hey are you with that boy who came in earlier, um, Luke Mudford?

COLIN: My kid brother.

DOCTOR 2: Bit of a pain, eh? Bloke gets a bit ignored when his kid brother's in hospital.

COLIN: You're not wrong. These really the keys for your car?

DOCTOR 2: Yep.

11

COLIN: Phew, radical.

DOCTOR 2: Look, don't worry about your brother. He'll be home in a couple of days.

COLIN: Prob'ly.

DOCTOR 2: Trust me. [*He retrieves his keys*] You don't get a car like this by being wrong. [*He goes.*]

COLIN: Yeah. Radical.

Mum is yelling down the phone to Iris in England.

MUM: Yes . . . Yes . . . No, he's fine. They've taken a blood sample . . . Tomorrow. We get the results tomorrow . . . Yes . . . Ambulance, that's right . . . No . . . No, completely out of the blue. One minute he was fine, next he was on the floor. . . The floor . . . The FLOOR . . . No, he had his Christmas dinner . . . Yes . . . Yes it is hot over here. I expect it's cold over there in Pommy-land . . . Snow? Oh, nice. . . . Yes . . . Yes we'll let you know. Love to Bob and little Alistair . . . Yes . . . Bye . . . Bye Iris . . . Yes . . . Bye love . . . Yes, you too. Bye.

Mum leaves.

In the hospital ward Luke, dressed in a hospital gown, gets set to bat. A Nurse sets a pile of bedpans for a wicket and gets down to catch. Colin enters running from off and bowls a beauty. Luke hits it off for six. From out of sight a loud matronly voice yells 'howzat!' Matron enters holding the ball between finger and thumb, her face sour.

12

NURSE: Shit!

The Nurse bundles Luke back into bed.

COLIN: It's alright, it's a soft ball. We're allowed to play with it indoors at home.

MATRON: [*to the Nurse*] Most irresponsible behaviour. This is a hospital, not the SCG. That child is very sick.

NURSE: Matron, the patient wasn't involved . . .

The bat falls out of Luke's bed.

MATRON: This will go on your report . . .

COLIN: You won't sack her willya? It wasn't her fault, besides a bit of cricket never hurt anyone . . .

Matron fixes him with a look that would stop a train and he retreats. Dad enters and the Matron talks quietly to him and then goes. Dad hovers over Luke, whispering earnestly and patting him awkwardly, while Colin composes a letter to Matron.

Dear Matron. Overseas, where they have the best hospitals in the world, cricket is often used to help patients get better. Spin bowling is good exercise for people who've done their wrists in, and batting is specially good for gastric because it strengthens the bowel muscles . . .

Dad approaches Colin looking very serious.

Oh-oh. I'm in it now. Em, did you see Luke's six, Dad? Reckon he must be almost better, eh?

DAD: Col, the hospital in Sydney that did tests on Luke's blood want to do some more. He has to go down there, today.

COLIN: Sydney! Far out. Are we all going down in the car?

DAD: That'd take too long. They're going to fly him down in the air ambulance this afternoon.

COLIN: A plane?! We're going to Sydney on a plane? Wow!

DAD: There's only room for one passenger so I'm going with him. You and Mum'll come down on the train tomorrow.

COLIN: Aw no! Da-ad!

Dad mistakes Colin's disappointment for worry about Luke.

DAD: I know it's a shock old mate. I'm worried sick myself. Um, you wanna say goodbye to your brother?

COLIN: See ya Luke.

LUKE: See ya Col.

The Nurse wheels Luke out.

DAD: Your Mum's a bit upset about it all, so I want you to look after her for me. Promise? [*Colin nods*]. We got to be tough. Alright, mate?

Dad follows Luke out. The Nurse re-enters and sol-

14

emnly picks up the bedpans and the cricket gear. She looks at Colin and smiles.

NURSE: It was a great six, but.

At home, Mum paces up and down. Colin enters the room carrying a plate and a fork.

COLIN: Sit down. Your tea's ready.

She sits. He watches anxiously as she pokes the fork into the meal.

MUM: It looks lovely. What is it?

COLIN: Curry.

MUM: Why is it green?

COLIN: It's pea curry.

MUM: Oh. She puts a bit in her mouth and chews.

COLIN: Is it good?

MUM: Very nice, love. Um, I like the glacé cherries.

COLIN: It's a sweet curry.

Mum puts some more in her mouth. Her face crumples and she fights back sobs.

Oh no. I didn't get all the lumps of curry powder out. I'll get you a drink of water.

He runs off. Mum composes herself. Colin returns and presses a glass of water in her hand.

MUM: Colin. There's something we haven't made clear to you about Luke.

COLIN: Your curry's getting cold.

MUM: The reason they've sent him to Sydney is because they think he might be pretty crook.

COLIN: Mum, stop worrying. You've seen those Sydney hospitals on telly; they got everything. They could cure a horse with its head on backwards down there. Come on, eat your curry.

MUM: Good on you Col.

COLIN: 'Member that show they had on every week about operations and stuff? That was from Sydney. 'Member the kid who swallowed her Dad's record player – not all at once, just bits of it and you could see all the bits on the X-ray and then they opened her up and found all the things her Mum and Dad had been lookin' for all year? Then there was that man whose heart went bung and they put a new one in, and the surgeon had it in his hand all bloody an beatin' all by itself – and remember the bloke who cut his foot off with the lawnmower and had it sewn back on? You're not eatin' your tea.

MUM: Sorry love, I'm not very hungry. Tired I expect.

COLIN: Put your feet up for a bit if you like.

MUM: Yeh, I might do that.

16

Mum puts her feet up and Colin picks up the plate of curry.

COLIN: I'll put this in the fridge. You might feel like it for breakfast. [*Mum smiles weakly.*]

Colin takes the plate away. He returns and covers Mum with a rug. She sniffs and tries to be brave. Colin lifts the rug and gets in beside her. He slips one arm under her neck and she snuggles against him. He wraps the rug round them both and hugs her tight. They turn the lights out. In the dark the phone rings and then stops.

Mum is carrying a bundle of Colin-size clothes. She starts folding them into a huge suitcase. Colin enters yawning.

COLIN: Morning Mum. Gor, you sure you're packin enough? They've probly got a kitchen sink in Sydney, you know.

MUM: This is not for Sydney.

COLIN: But them's my clothes.

MUM: Colin, your Dad rung from the Sydney hospital last night. Him and me . . . We'd like you to go and stay with Uncle Bob and Auntie Iris in England for a bit.

COLIN: Wha . . .?

MUM: We're not going to make you go. But we'd like you to. For your sake and for ours.

COLIN: I can't go to England – cricket practice starts next week.

MUM: You'll have a great time over there. Uncle Bob and Auntie Iris live near London Zoo and Uncle Bob goes to the cricket all the time. And little Alistair, your cousin, he's practically your age.

COLIN: What'd I do . . .?

MUM: Oh love, it's not that. It's just for the best. The doctors say Luke isn't going to get better.

COLIN: From gastric? People always get better from gastric!

MUM: It's not gastric. They showed Dad the X-rays. It's . . . It's . . .

COLIN: No! I can be a help to you! I can make the tea so you can look after him. I can bring him his homework from school. You don't have to send me away!

MUM: Colin, a terrible thing's happening and we don't want you to have to suffer too.

COLIN: What terrible thing? What's so terrible you have to send me away?

MUM: Don't you understand! Luke's got cancer! He's going to die!

She rushes out. Colin shouts after her.

COLIN: Bull! I don't believe you! They're bein' slack! If they can sew a bloke's foot on and put a new heart in somebody surely they can cure a bit of cancer! [*He starts to throw his clothes angrily out of the suitcase.*] What about the man in the newsagents? He had cancer on his head and they cured him. Expect me to believe that you can get the cricket from India and get bombs that could blow the whole world up and robots and space ships and they can't cure a bit of cancer! Bull! They're just not tryin'! [*He slumps down.*] Bloody slack. If it was somebody important they'd pull their finger out alright. If it was the Prime Minister they'd be askin' the Queen of England for the world's best doctor's phone number then, eh? I bet the Queen has the world's best doctor right there beside her in London. London! [*He starts throwing the clothes back in the suitcase. He picks it up and leaves the room.*] Hey Mum. What time's my plane?

Colin, Mum and Dad are waiting at the airport for the plane to board.

COLIN: You don't have to worry. Everything's going to be OK.

DAD: Good on ya, Col.

COLIN: No, I mean, Luke isn't going to die.

DAD: Don't son.

COLIN: Mum, are you listening? I said, Luke isn't going to die.

MUM: [*sharply*] Don't talk about things you don't understand.

COLIN: I do understand.

DAD: Colin, it's not up to us.

19

COLIN: I know. That's what I'm trying to explain.

MUM: [*too brightly*] Why don't you think about all the exciting things you're going to do with Uncle Bob and Auntie Iris and Alistair.

COLIN: Stack me, some people don't want to be cheered up! Mum, I'm trying to tell you about Luke.

MUM: Don't talk about it. Please don't.

Dad takes him aside while Mum composes herself.

DAD: We've got to be strong old mate, and cop it on the chin.

COLIN: But Dad . . .

DAD: Now, when you write to Luke, don't say anything about . . . You know.

COLIN: The cancer.

DAD: The doctors haven't and we've decided not to. Don't want him scared on top of everything.

COLIN: Don't worry, I won't say anything about him dying, cos he's not going to.

MUM: [*joining them again*] Be a good boy for Uncle Bob and Auntie Iris, won't you? It was kind of them to help out with the ticket and everything.

COLIN: Yeh, yeh.

A flight attendant approaches.

FLIGHT ATT: Colin Mudford?

MUM: Yes, this is Colin.

FLIGHT ATT: I'm your flight attendant. I'll be looking after you on the plane.

COLIN: Let's go.

FLIGHT ATT: We'll get you boarded then.

MUM: Oh, your passport – here, and some English money. It's not much, but . . .

COLIN: I won't need much.

MUM: It's for the best, love. We'll send for you soon – once it's all . . . When it's all . . .

DAD: We'll leave you to it then, son.

FLIGHT ATT: Don't worry, we'll see him right.

MUM: And keep warm, won't you?

Colin embraces Mum.

COLIN: [*to Dad*] Don't worry, I got it all worked out. I got a plan.

LOUDSPEAKER VOICE: This is your boarding call for Qantas flight number one to London via Melbourne and Singapore. Now boarding at gate ten, Qantas flight number one to London via Melbourne and Singapore.

The attendant takes Colin to his seat.

FLIGHT ATT: This is your call button. If you need a drink or anything, just press it. Someone will come round with headphones and there'll be a movie later.

COLIN: This is great. How long is it?

FLIGHT ATT: Oh, twenty four hours or so.

COLIN: No, the plane, not the flight.

FLIGHT ATT: Oh, sorry. [*She tells him in metres.*]

COLIN: You know, that's long enough for an indoor cricket pitch. If you moved all the seats out down one side you could have one, then all your passengers would get the exercise which would counteract the effects of jet lag.

FLIGHT ATT: I'll pass that on to the Captain.

A grim-faced businessman rushes in late and sits beside Colin. The attendant goes through the usual vacuous safety routine to the unintelligible voice on the intercom. The noise of the plane taxi-ing for take-off is heard. Throughout the flight, the businessman tries to ignore Colin.

COLIN: [*to the businessman*] Lifejackets! Great. You think we better get ours out? You'd be right. In the water, I mean. Got enough fat on you to keep you warm. I'd be a gonner. [*The noise rises in pitch*] Woa, some speed eh? Did you know most plane crashes happen on take-off? [*They lean back as the plane takes off.*] Hey, there's Sydney harbour bridge. Isn't it beautiful? My brother's in Sydney, in hospital. You reckon they're

22

all lookin' up at us while we're lookin' down? I bet him and all the Nurses are lookin' out the hospital window at us. Wave, go on, just in case. I bet he's ropable, he only got to go in the air ambulance, I'm in a jumbo. Boo sucks Lukey mate!

Later.

Gor, they don't half feed you a lot. I'm as stuffed as a Christmas turkey.

The businessman gives a grunt of pain.

Is that a bit of cancer?

BUSINESSMAN: I beg your pardon?

COLIN: Cancer. It's where the cells start growing too fast inside your body and your whole system can go bung. I've been reading up on it.

BUSINESSMAN: I know what it is. I just don't particularly want to talk about it.

COLIN: Funny that. My folks are the same. Why not?

BUSINESSMAN: Because it's not a very pleasant topic.

COLIN: There's worse topics. [*He thinks*] Like nuclear war and why sick has bits in it. [*The businessman groans.*] Only, if you've got it, I'd have it seen to.

BUSINESSMAN: I haven't got it! I've got indigestion.

COLIN: Mum always gets indigestion if she bolts her tucker.

Later.

You want a go at doing this quiz? Which Prime Minister played cricket for Australia? No? Do you want to colour in this picture of a Koala? The crayons are a bit crappy but it was good of the Hostie to give it to me.

The Captain and the attendant appear.

CAPTAIN: G'day Colin. Thought you might like a look at the flight deck.

COLIN: Too right! [*He stands*]

BUSINESSMAN: Excuse me miss, do you have any other seats available?

COLIN: Oh, don't worry. I'm going up to the flight deck, so you can have both seats for a while.

CAPTAIN: So. We're travelling to London by ourselves, eh?

COLIN: Well, I am.

CAPTAIN: And what are you going to do in London?

COLIN: I'm going to see the Queen.

CAPTAIN: The Queen, eh? [*He winks at the attendant.*] Going to drop in for tea and cucumber sandwiches are you?

COLIN: No. I'm going to ask her to help cure my brother's cancer.

CAPTAIN: Ar, em, yes, well . . .

Later.

COLIN: [*returning to his seat*] You should see the
equipment and all the dials and lights and
everything. Here we are, in a plane bigger than
Myers up in the air sixty thousand feet over
Dubrovnik; if modern technology can do this, it can
cure cancer standing on its head. What do you
reckon.

Later.

And then Arnie Strachan told me that when his
Uncle died they put his ashes in a box and sent them
to his rellies in England. Only, they put him in the
same parcel as things to put in the Christmas cake,
so the rellies thought his Uncle's ashes was some new
kind of spices and they put him in the Christmas
cake, cos they sent the letter separate, see, and the
letter didn't get there until after the cake was made.
And the letter said that his Uncle wanted to be buried
at sea, so they took the cake out on the ferry and
chucked bits of it in the water, only these seagulls
kept swooping and carrying bits of him off.
Anyway . . .

Later. Colin is sound asleep.

FLIGHT ATT: Ladies and gentlemen. We hope you had a
pleasant flight. The temperature at Heathrow is
minus two degrees, and the time is five fifteen p.m.
Please remain in your seats until the aircraft has
taxied to a complete halt. We ask that you take care
when opening overhead lockers as luggage may fall
out and cause injury. Exit will be through the forward
door only. Thank you for choosing to fly Qantas. We

hope we can be of service to you again when next you travel.

The businessman leaves looking like death. The attendant wakes Colin and takes him off the plane.

Colin yawns and stretches, looks around and shivers. The attendant returns with his suitcase and a notice on a stick with his name in large letters.

FLIGHT ATT: Just wait here for them. They can't miss you.

COLIN: What if they don't come?

FLIGHT ATT: They will.

COLIN: But what if they don't?

FLIGHT ATT: [*winking*] Then I'll take you home with me, eh?

COLIN: I wouldn't mind.

FLIGHT ATT: Watch it! Anyway, I'll come back and check in five minutes, just in case. See ya, Colin Mudford. [*She goes*]

COLIN: See ya. [*He waits*] Wonder what they're like? I hope they're understanding types. [*He practices telling them*] Nice to meet you Uncle Bob and aunty Iris, but I've really come to London to meet the Queen. [*He answers himself as Uncle Bob.*] Oh, is that right young man? Well, if our 'ot dinners and spare bed aren't good enough for you, you can rack off!

26

Bob, Iris and Alistair arrive.

IRIS: I told you we'd be late. Stop sniffing Alistair. [*Alistair sniffs*].

BOB: You heard your mother.

IRIS: We should have parked in the airport carpark.

BOB: I'm not parking in that car park.

IRIS: Alistair, where's your hanky?

BOB: The way they charge to park a car.

IRIS: Well, we're late now, you and your car park.

BOB: They're not getting it out of me. I can tell you that much.

IRIS: There he is! Hello Colin love.

There are hello's and handshakes and kisses all round.

Well. Just look at you. How's your Mum?

COLIN: She's good.

IRIS: And your Dad?

COLIN: Good.

IRIS: Alistair don't stand like that, love. It's bad for your spine.

COLIN: Luke's a bit crook, but.

IRIS: Um, yes, well. Alistair!

ALISTAIR: Sorry.

BOB: I'm not paying for you to have your posture straightened.

IRIS: Well! Shall we be off then?

COLIN: Just a tick.

Colin opens his suitcase and pulls out a jumper. He puts it on. Then he pulls out several more and puts them on.

Right. [*They leave*]

Colin is being shown the spare bed in Alistair's bedroom.

IRIS: This is your bed. I hope you'll be comfortable, love. You'll soon get 'climatised. Don't pick your scalp Alistair.

BOB: I expect you'll be wanting to see the sights, soon as you've got over your jet lag.

ALISTAIR: The Zoo's good.

IRIS: Big Ben. Alistair!

BOB: You heard your mother. You'll get scabs, you will.

COLIN: I want to go to Buckingham Palace.

BOB: What would you want to go to that dump for?

IRIS: Er . . . now what else is there . . .?

BOB: Waste of tax-payer's money, that place. Ought to be pulled down.

IRIS: Madame Tussaud's?

COLIN: Well, not the palace really. It's the Queen I want to see.

ALISTAIR: Oh-oh.

BOB: Don't you talk to me about the Queen!

IRIS: Alright Bob . . .

BOB: Get me started on the Queen . . .

IRIS: Don't mind Uncle Bob, love. He's got a bit of a thing about, you know, them.

ALISTAIR: Thinks they should be stuffed and put in a museum.

IRIS: Alright thank you, Alistair. [To Colin] We don't go into the city much, as a rule. But don't worry, Alistair here will show you all the sights, won't you love?

ALISTAIR: Will I?

IRIS: Go on love, show him.

ALISTAIR: Huh?

IRIS: Get it out and show him.

ALISTAIR: Oh, yeh. [*He gets out a picture book.*]

IRIS: Got everything in there. London Bridge, Hyde Park. Lovely colours.

ALISTAIR: And the Royal family.

BOB: Talk to me about the bloomin' Queen . . .

IRIS: We'll have a bit of an outing tomorrow, if it's nice.

BOB: Good idea.

IRIS: Do you good. Take your mind off . . . the flight and . . .

BOB: Things.

COLIN: Great.

BOB: Tell you what. Tomorrow after work, we'll take you to the biggest do-it-yourself hardware centre in Greater London.

COLIN: Great.

BOB: We were a bit worried when they first built it, but it's the focal point of the district now.

IRIS: Yes, we're very pleased with it. Do you know, it's bigger than Fulham football ground.

COLIN: Mmmmm.

BOB: Got everything in there for the home improvements. Nothing's too small or too big. And videos running to show you how to do things, like.

Colin yawns.

IRIS: Oh look, he's tired. We'll let you have an early night love, eh?

COLIN: No, it's not that. It's just that I'm finding it a bit hard to concentrate on hardware at the moment while Luke's got cancer.

IRIS: Yes, um, well I think an early night for all of us. Leave that alone, Alistair.

ALISTAIR: I wasn't . . .

BOB: You heard your mother.

IRIS: We won't wake you in the morning love. Let you have a lie in. Alistair's coming to work with me tomorrow so I can take him to the doctor's.

ALISTAIR: I'm sickening for something.

BOB: You make yourself right at home tomorrow.

IRIS: There's the telly and the radio and Uncle Bob's do-it-yourself magazines . . .

BOB: The important thing is to relax and take your mind completely off, you know . . . things.

COLIN: Thanks.

IRIS: Nighty-night then. Don't forget your teeth, Alistair.

They start to leave, whispering.

Did you hear him? He said it right out. Couldn't believe my ears.

BOB: He's a bit of a funny one alright.

IRIS: Right out loud . . . [*They go*].

Alistair gets undressed and puts his pj's on.

ALISTAIR: You nearly got him started on the Queen.

COLIN: What's he got against her?

ALISTAIR: I don't know. Something about how she never had to get her hands dirty.

COLIN: Well, she wouldn't would she? She's the Queen.

ALISTAIR: Yeh.

COLIN: Where exactly is Buckingham Palace?

ALISTAIR: In town. Miles away.

COLIN: How do you get there?

ALISTAIR: Quickest way's by tube, but it's pretty dangerous. You have to get in the same carriage as dozens of other people. You can catch cold, or flu, or anything. Well, not anything. A lot of things, but not, you know, anything.

COLIN: It's OK Alistair. I know you don't catch cancer from other people.

ALISTAIR: Mum said that word wasn't to be mentioned in this house.

COLIN: What word?

ALISTAIR: That word.

COLIN: Cancer?

ALISTAIR: Shooosh!

IRIS: [*from out of sight*] Lights out boys.

ALISTAIR: Aren't you going to put your pyjamas on?

COLIN: Um, what's the temperature get down to round here?

ALISTAIR: Don't know. Never took much notice.

Colin looks at his pj's, takes off one jumper and puts the pj's on top of his clothes.

COLIN: Night then.

ALISTAIR: Er . . . Yeh.

People are rushing about in noisy London town. Some are in arab clothing, there is the occasional bowler and umbrella. Colin enters bewildered and wide eyed.

COLIN: 'Scuse me . . .'Scuse . . . Could you tell me which train goes to Buckingham Palace. 'Scuse me?

Everybody ignores him. He rushes about trying to get someone to answer him. Finally the crowd mills around him in an organic mass. Colin cannot escape. The mass takes him on a tube. They rattle along hanging on to straps.

Could you tell me please where to get off for
Buckingham Palace? 'Scuse me.

*Colin struggles to get a map out and tries to read it to
no avail. Suddenly the crowd lurches as the tube stops
and the mass carries Colin off the tube. Then they all
scatter in different directions. Colin is alone. A huge set
of wrought iron gates appear. He does not see them and
yells out.*

Would someone please tell me how to get to
Buckingham Palace!!!! [*He notices the gates.*] Oh.
Right. Good one.

*As Colin peers through the gates, a guard in red tunic and tall
bearskin hat appears. The guard spends most of the next few
minutes repressing an intense desire to laugh.*

COLIN: G'day. [*The guard does not respond.*] Geez, they're
a friendly mob round here. 'Scuse me. I'm here to
see the Queen?

A tourist or two wander up.

AMERICAN TOURIST: Hey, kid. You're in my picture.

COLIN: [*to guard*] Please tell the Queen that Colin
Mudford is here from Australia.

SPANISH TOURIST: [*grinning*] And Manuel Corbes from
Madrid.

COLIN: I need her Majesty's help. Hello? [*No response.*]
Maybe it's my accent. [*He tries to sound posh*] It is an
urgent medical matter. My . . . brother . . . Luke . . .

34

has . . . got . . . a . . . serious . . . medical . . .
condition.

The guard twitches.

AMERICAN: That don't give you the right to mess up other people's photo opportunities.

COLIN: Just let me in and I'll explain inside.

SPANIARD: Me too.

COLIN: Look. I know you're probably not meant to open the gate and you probably get people lying through their teeth all the time, but I promise you I'm telling the truth and if you open the gate I'll explain everything to the Queen and you won't lose your job or get sent to Northern Ireland.

The guard nearly loses control. A policeman enters behind Colin, who loses his temper.

You'd better open that gate, cos when the Queen finds out you've kept a sick kid waiting, she's gunna do you!

The policeman collars Colin.

POLICEMAN: Now then, son. What seems to be the problem?

COLIN: At last. Well, I need to see the Queen.

POLICEMAN: You do, do you?

COLIN: Yes. And I reckon this bloke's a bit deaf or . . .

you know [*He makes loony gestures.*] . . . something. So
if you could just unlock the gate for me.

POLICEMAN: Unlock the gate.

COLIN: Yes, thanks.

POLICEMAN: [*laughing*] That's a good one. Unlock the
gate, eh?

COLIN: If you wouldn't mind. I need to see the Queen
about my sick brother.

SPANIARD: And my sick mother.

POLICEMAN: Do yourself a favour, and write her a letter
about it, cos if I see you hanging around here again,
you'll be the one who's feeling sick. [*He roars*] Gotit!?
Now push off. [*Colin pushes off.*] Who does he think
he is? Barry Bleedin Mckenzie?

SPANIARD: Que?

*A squeak escapes from the guard. The policeman turns
to check him out. The guard is stoney-faced.*

Colin reads from the letter he has just written.

COLIN: Dear your Majesty the Queen. I need to speak to
you urgently about my brother Luke. He's got
cancer and the doctors in Australia are being really
slack. If I could borrow your top doctor for a while I
know he/she would fix things up in no time. Of
course Mum and Dad would pay his/her fares even
if it meant selling the car or getting a loan. Please
contact me at the above address urgently. Yours

36

sincerely, Colin Mudford. PS. This is not a hoax. Ring the above number and Auntie Iris will tell you. Hang up if a man answers. [*He puts it in an envelope and looks at it.*] Two days, I reckon. Three tops.

Iris and Bob are putting coats and scarves on, getting ready to go to work.

IRIS: Now Alistair, take two kelp tablets every four hours with water and one vitamin C tablet every two hours with milk and no running around. Ooh, is that the post?

ALISTAIR: I'll get it.

Colin flies past him, returns with it and leafs anxiously through the letters.

IRIS: Don't fret love. You've only been here a week, it takes at least that for a letter to come from Australia.

BOB: Don't talk to me about letters.

IRIS: Bit homesick, are you pet?

BOB: What about that Christmas card? Came from Cheshire via Israel.

IRIS: You can give Mum and Dad a quick ring if you like, just the once.

COLIN: No, it's OK, I'm fine. Thanks anyway.

IRIS: Now, stay indoors with your chest Alistair. Lunch is in the fridge. Bye loves.

BOB: You heard your mother. Ta-ta then. [*They go*]

ALISTAIR: Colin?

COLIN: What?

ALISTAIR: Have you really ridden a trail bike, or were you pulling my leg?

COLIN: Straight up. Yamaha 250. Twin exhaust, cross-country gear ratios.

ALISTAIR: Brill.

COLIN: Yeh, it was alright till the brakes failed and I went over the cliff.

ALISTAIR: You went over a cliff?

COLIN: Yeh. But it's OK, the ocean was underneath, broke my fall.

ALISTAIR: The Pacific Ocean?

COLIN: Yeh. The surf wasn't too high, only fifteen metres or so.

ALISTAIR: Brill.

COLIN: 'Course the sharks were a problem.

ALISTAIR: Sharks!

COLIN: White pointers. There were a couple of them. Reminded me of the time I had to fight crocs off in the Territory.

ALISTAIR: Crocodiles?

COLIN: Twenty-footers. I gave them a wrestle for their money, but.

ALISTAIR: Do you know Crocodile Dundee?

COLIN: He's a mate of mine, gave me a few tips. See, a croc's got no brains. You can outsmart 'em. Not like sharks. Only way with sharks is to out-swim them.

ALISTAIR: You can out-swim sharks?

COLIN: All Australians can. Wouldn't be any of us left if we couldn't. Alistair, don't you ever get bored?

ALISTAIR: No. Well, a bit. Sometimes.

COLIN: How would you like to help me save Luke's life?

ALISTAIR: I'm not allowed to give blood!

COLIN: You don't have to give blood. Listen, do you reckon the Queen's doctor would be the best doctor in the world?

ALISTAIR: Yes, pretty good, specially cos he'd have to do it without looking.

COLIN: Eh?

ALISTAIR: Well, he would, wouldn't he? I mean if the Queen was sick he couldn't just say, 'take your frock off your Majesty and let me look at your . . . er . . . your . . . you know', could he? I mean, not the Queen. Nobody could, could they? He'd have to guess what's wrong. He'd have to be good.

COLIN: Er . . . yeh. Anyway, I wrote to her and asked her to let me get in touch with him, and she didn't write back.

ALISTAIR: When did you write to her?

COLIN: Nearly a week ago.

ALISTAIR: Well, there you are then. It'll be months before she gets round to it.

COLIN: She a bit slack?

ALISTAIR: No, not her. But hundreds of people write to her. She gets sackfuls of letters every day. Special vans full of letters for her.

COLIN: I've seen them. They've got Royal Mail written on them.

ALISTAIR: Er, yeh. Takes a bit of time to answer all them letters.

COLIN: Well, I haven't got time, I'm going to have to get into the palace and talk to her myself. And you're gonna help me.

ALISTAIR: You want me to help you break into Buckingham Palace?!

COLIN: Someone has to give me a leg up.

ALISTAIR: Mum doesn't let me go into town by myself.

COLIN: You won't be by yourself, you'll be with me.

ALISTAIR: But you can't just climb into the palace, there'll be alarms and dogs and stuff.

COLIN: No there won't, well only corgis and they'll be asleep on the Queen's bed.

ALISTAIR: How do you know?

COLIN: It was in our papers at home. A few years ago, a bloke got into Buckingham Palace at night and next morning, when the Queen woke up he was sitting on the end of her bed, looking at her. He didn't have a single dog bite on him.

ALISTAIR: I remember that.

COLIN: If he can do it, we can.

ALISTAIR: They put him in a loony bin.

COLIN: Alright then! I'll do it myself.

ALISTAIR: I'll come.

COLIN: OK, we'll set the alarm tonight for three-thirty in the morning.

ALISTAIR: I'll stay.

COLIN: Don't be a wimp.

ALISTAIR: What if you get shot?

COLIN: OK stay then!

ALISTAIR: I'll come.

COLIN: Good one. Three-thirty then. Let's go and buy a rope. [*They start to go.*]

ALISTAIR: But I'm not allowed out in the traffic.

COLIN: Alistair, anybody'd think a bus was gonna jump the kerb and weave through all the other shoppers, carefully avoiding rubbish bins and brick walls and flatten you!

ALISTAIR: Well, one could do, couldn't it?

COLIN: Alright, I'll go and buy the rope myself.

ALISTAIR: I'll come.

It is three-thirty in the morning. The gates of the palace appear through the darkness. The boys appear, Colin has his map.

COLIN: I know the palace is round here somewhere.

ALISTAIR: We're lost, I knew we'd get lost.

COLIN: We're not lost.

ALISTAIR: How do you know?

COLIN: Cos I know!

ALISTAIR: It could take days to find us. We could starve. If we don't die from the pollution.

COLIN: I'll put you on the bus home if you like.

ALISTAIR: I'll come.

COLIN: Right.

ALISTAIR: What if she wakes up and sees you sitting there and gets such a fright she wets the bed? Do you know how many years in jail you'd get for making the Queen wet the bed?

COLIN: I'm not gunna break into her bedroom, dumbo! I'll wait in one of the toilets and pop into the dining room and have a word when she's at breakfast.

A policeman strolls past. Alistair whimpers. The policeman stops and listens. Colin grabs him and pulls him into the shadows. The policeman ambles off, muttering something about corgis.

Right! Let's have that rope.

Alistair opens his anorak, underneath a rope is coiled round him. They uncoil it. Colin tries to lasso the top of the gates.

ALISTAIR: Hurry up! Pretend it's one of them crocodiles.

Colin manages to lasso a spike on top of the gate. He tugs on the rope to test it.

COLIN: Right, give us a leg-up.

Alistair has obviously never given anyone a leg-up before and there is much struggling and falling over. Finally Alistair hoists Colin up halfway.

ALISTAIR: Oh my God, oh my God, oh my God.

COLIN: Oh no. Here we go, he's going to panic now.

ALISTAIR: Oh my God, oh my God.

COLIN: Alistair! You right down there?

ALISTAIR: Alright? Alright? We're breaking into Buckingham Palace! Sodding brilliant!

COLIN: Onya Alistair! Let's go!

Alistair heaves Colin up as far as he can. Colin keeps on climbing up the rope. Suddenly a brilliant spotlight flashes on them.

ALISTAIR: Oh my God, oh my God, oh my God!

All hell breaks loose. Sirens wail, bells ring, cops come running. Colin, atop the gates, pinned in the light, freezes.

COLIN: Oh, shit!

The police have brought the boys home to Iris and Bob's place.

IRIS: This is the thanks we get for taking you into our home. Alistair! Stop snivelling!

BOB: We're in the computer now! The whole family in the police computer.

IRIS: Out all night!

BOB: Do you know how lucky you are? You could have been charged!

IRIS: You could have been killed! 'Specially you, Alistair.

BOB: I'm not having any more trouble from you two. I'll be locking those doors when we go to work!

COLIN: That won't stop me! The Queen will get to my letter one day and then she'll come round here with a tank and bash the door down!

BOB: No she flippin' won't!

COLIN: Yes she bloody will.

IRIS: Ooh! Language. Alistair, up the stairs with you this minute. Talk to him Bob. [*She leaves with Alistair.*] Never heard such cheek in my life. Use your hanky!

BOB: You can forget the Queen, Colin my lad. She hasn't got time for the likes of you and Luke.

COLIN: Bull! I've seen them on the telly visiting sick people and stuff – even lepers.

BOB: Well, what good did it ever do a leper to have his hand shook by royalty? He's still a leper. They don't leave any of their money behind on his bedside table, do they?

COLIN: She's got to help me, she's got to.

BOB: Colin, if the Queen bothered herself with solving other people's problems there would be a queue from Buckingham Palace to our back door. Don't you know why she locks herself in behind those gates?

COLIN: 'Course I do, it's to keep burglars out.

BOB: To keep burglars out, and to keep her from having to bother with the likes of us!

45

COLIN: But people can write to her, then she doesn't have to see them and tire herself out, then she can help them.

BOB: Believe me, she won't even read your letter.

COLIN: She will.

BOB: Think about it lad, you know she won't.

COLIN: Well, what's she there for if she doesn't help people? What's all that money and all those cars and houses and armies and stuff for?

BOB: She's there, crippling us with taxes to keep her in the lap of luxury just so we can point to her and say we got a Queen.

COLIN: That's not much use to anyone.

BOB: You hit the nail on the head there, lad. Nope, if you've got something needs fixing, take a leaf out of my book and do it yourself.

COLIN: [*thoughtfully*] Do it yourself . . .

BOB: Stand you in good stead if you remember that. Don't see me running to the Queen every time my roof leaks or my car breaks down or I get in the police computer, do you?

COLIN: Yeh . . . do it yourself!

BOB: Only way, lad.

COLIN: Bugger the Queen, eh?

BOB: Yes, well. Um . . . Watch your language around
   your auntie Iris eh?

COLIN: Yeh, alright.

BOB: Better get yourself a bit of shut-eye then.

COLIN: Yeh.

They leave.

*Alistair is in his room. He is tying a lasso knot in his dressing-
gown cord and practising his throw. Colin enters carrying a
phone book.*

ALISTAIR: Have they gone to work?

COLIN: Just.

ALISTAIR: Have they locked us in?

COLIN: Tight as a chook's bum. You even got locks on
   your windows in your house.

ALISTAIR: Yeh, well, can't be too careful.

COLIN: Hey, what you reckon the best cancer hospital in
   London would be under – H for hospital, or C for
   cancer?

ALISTAIR: R.

COLIN: What?

ALISTAIR: For Royal. Everything important here's called
   the Royal something.

COLIN: There's the Royal Children's Hospital . . . The Royal Automobile Club . . . Royal Bar and Grill . . . Royale Fish Shop . . . No Royal Cancer Hospital.

ALISTAIR: Try under Her Majesty's.

COLIN: [*looking*] Nuh. No cancer hospital.

ALISTAIR: Try under Queen Elizabeth.

COLIN: I reckon I'll just go out and find it. Got a screwdriver?

ALISTAIR: What for?

COLIN: To take the lock off the back door.

ALISTAIR: You can't do that! They'll go bananas.

COLIN: I'll be back before they are and I'll put it back on – they'll never know.

ALISTAIR: Well, you can't. All the tools are outside in the garage.

COLIN: Not to worry. [*He pulls out his Swiss army knife and leaves.*]

ALISTAIR: No! Don't! We'll get killed! That's a new lock that is! From the biggest hardware centre in Greater London. They'll kill us. I'm not supposed to be having stress. What about my dandruff? [*He rubs his head and checks out the dandruff.*] Oooohhh. It's stress that does it. I'll be out in a rash next and Mum'll kill me. I'll be having an asthma attack, sure to. [*He wheezes.*]

Colin re-enters with the lock and chucks it at Alistair who catches it as though it was red-hot and throws it back. Alistair leaps into his bed and pulls the cover over his head.

I don't care! Do what you like! I don't want to know! I can't see a thing – don't know anything.

COLIN: See ya, Alistair.

ALISTAIR: On your own head be it!

Colin carefully places the lock on the top of the mound of blankets which is Alistair's head and goes.

A row of patients in wheelchairs are lined up like dummies for inspection by student doctors to the sound of loud pompous music. A puffed-up, suave and distinguished looking male doctor enters. Colin enters and a Nurse approaches him.

NURSE: You lost luv?

COLIN: Is this the best cancer hospital in London?

NURSE: It's the best in the world.

COLIN: I'm not lost then.

NURSE: That's good. [*She goes back to the patients.*]

DOCTOR: [*holding up a patient's hand to feel the pulse and speaking in a plummy voice*] Accessibility is paramount. [*The students scribble in their notepads*] The patient must always feel that he can speak to you, that you have time for him. [*To patient*] And how are we today? [*There is no reply from the patient, the doctor drops the hand.*] That's the ticket. Next? [*He moves to the next patient and has a listen through his stethoscope. He shouts in the patient's ear.*] Feeling better are we? [*There is no reply.*] Good, good. [*He starts to move to the next one.*]

COLIN: 'Scuse me butting in . . . [*The doctor sweeps past him.*] I know you're real busy here and everything, but I'd really appreciate it if you'd come to Australia and fix Luke up. They reckon he's gunna die, but I reckon they're just slack and you could fix him.

DOCTOR: Who is this?

COLIN: Luke, my brother.

DOCTOR: I mean, who is this boy?

The student doctors look at one another in alarm. One of them looks at his note-pad.

COLIN: We'll pay your fare. Or if you've got a jet of your own we'll pay the petrol.

DOCTOR: Remove this! At once!

The students try to grab Colin. He runs rings round them.

COLIN: You got to help, Luke's got cancer, he could die!

DOCTOR: Everyone here has got cancer! They could all die!!

There is a big silence, one student clears his throat, another studies his toe-caps. The patients' heads swivel in unison towards the doctor.

50

DOCTOR: If your brother has got . . . [*He lowers his voice for the word*] cancer, there are proper channels.

COLIN: Please . . . just listen to me for a minute . . .

DOCTOR: I will not have my ward round disrupted like this!

COLIN: You've got to do it. It'll only take you a few days. You've got to!

DOCTOR: Out! Out with him at once!

The doctor leaves, the students and the Nurse wheel out the remaining patients.

COLIN: [*yelling*] You know what you are? You're the worst doctor in the world, you hear me? The worst doctor in the world! [*He starts to cry and then pulls himself together.*] Alright Colin mate, don't start blubbering. Dad wouldn't blubber. Not even the time you bowled a Malcolm Marshall special off an extra long run-up and it bounced off a cow pat and slammed him in the privates. Nothin' to blubber about. You went for the wrong doctor, that's all. Just because he looked like the world's best doctor. The real world's best doctor's probably bald with glasses. I just got to get back in there and find him.

As Colin speaks, a man [Ted] enters some little distance away and begins to cry. Colin shuffles about a bit, embarrassed and then approaches.

COLIN: You OK?

TED: No.

51

COLIN: Oh, right.

TED: [*looking up and trying to smile*] But ta for asking. [*He blows his nose*] I needed that.

COLIN: Why?

TED: I've got a . . . friend in there who's very sick. Normally I cope, but once a week I treat myself to a bit of a cry.

COLIN: Cancer?

Ted looks at Colin as if he is about to say something, then nods.

TED: You the one who was making all that commotion?

COLIN: Colin Mudford.

TED: Ted Caldicot. What were you doing, pinching old ladies' grapes?

COLIN: No. Trying to find a doctor for my brother, only I found the wrong one.

TED: Has your brother got cancer?

COLIN: At last!

TED: What?

COLIN: A grown-up who isn't scared to say that word.

TED: What, cancer?

COLIN: Yeah, cancer.

TED: Cancer cancer cancer cancer cancer.

COLIN: Cancer cancer cancer cancer cancer.

They start to laugh.

COLIN: I'm as dry as a creek at Christmas.

TED: Pardon?

COLIN: I'm thirsty.

TED: There's a caff here in the hospital.

COLIN: My shout.

TED: Huh?

COLIN: I'm buying.

TED: You're on!

In the hospital cafeteria there are a few tables and a woman in a hospital volunteer uniform. Ted and Colin approach and sit at a table. Ted is still laughing. A few miserable looking people sit at other tables.

You actually climbed the gates of Buckingham Palace! Colin, you're an inspiration. You're better than a doctor. [*The woman approaches*] Six chocolate frogs please, love.

COLIN: Six chocolate frogs?!

TED: Wait and see.

COLIN: What's that say on your hand?

TED: This? It's Welsh. It means forever.

COLIN: That's nice. Nicer than a picture of a snake or love and hate tattooed on your fingers.

TED: Where I come from in Wales, people get them done when they're in love.

COLIN: Oh yeh? Has your friend got one then?

TED: Yes, my friend's got one. [*The woman puts a box on the table.*]

WOMAN: There's ten left in the box.

TED: I'd better take the lot, then. [*He gives the woman some money*] Hold these, Colin. [*Ted addresses the people in the cafe.*] Excuse me ladies and gentlemen. Excuse me. If you could see your faces. What a load of misery-guts. Look, we're all here for the same reason. We've all got people in there who need us very much. What they don't need is to look at a load of miserable faces. So, if anyone here thinks they might be turning into a misery-guts, I'd strongly recommend a chocolate frog from my young friend here.

The people in the cafe look at Ted and Colin like they are mad. Colin looks really embarrassed. He offers the frogs round. After a moment someone takes one. The tension is broken, people smile and accept a frog.

WOMAN: I'll have to order some more of those in.

TED: Tell you what. [*He hands Colin a pen and paper*] Write down the name of the hospital Luke's in for me.

COLIN: Why?

TED: I know a couple of doctors here pretty well. They're top people. I could have a word with them about Luke.

COLIN: Ripper. I mean yes – please.

TED: OK. Why don't you meet me here, say Wednesday at midday, we'll go see them.

COLIN: Could we make it tomorrow? I'm in a bit of a hurry.

TED: I'll do my best.

Colin is shouting down the phone to his Mum in Australia.

Yes, yes, Auntie Iris said I could, just this once . . . No, no you get used to the cold. How's Luke . . . Oh . . . Well it won't be for much longer . . . No, you don't understand. See, I got great news . . . No . . . Yes . . . Mum, listen to me a minute . . . Listen! I'm going to see one of London's top cancer doctors. Tomorrow. Luke's going to be cured . . . Are you there? Mum? Your voice sounds funny . . . Did you hear what I said? I'm fixing it up tomorrow. It's all going to be alright now . . . Don't cry . . . Let go of what? I can't understand a word you're saying. [*Bob enters*] I better go. Uncle Bob's pointing at his watch. Bye Mum, see you all soon. Bye.

BOB: Alright then?

COLIN: She always cries when she's happy.

Bob puts his arm round Colin's shoulders.

In Alistair's bedroom. Colin is punching numbers on a mobile phone.

ALISTAIR: You won't get away with it again, you know.

COLIN: Hello, Qantas? Could you tell me please which days this week you've got empty seats for Australia?

ALISTAIR: You fluked it yesterday, but if you take that lock off again, they'll find out.

COLIN: No, it's not a school project . . .

ALISTAIR: I'm warning you . . .

COLIN: Shush a minute. Now, they can't be near the dunnies, one of the passengers is a very eminent doctor. I see, you never put eminent doctors near the dunnies. That's good.

ALISTAIR: We'll be eating cold baked beans for a week.

COLIN: Shurrup! No, sorry, not you. Yes, thank you very much. I'll let you know. Bye. [*Colin takes out his Swiss army knife and holds it up and winks at Alistair*] See ya Alistair.

Alistair makes a lunge for the knife. They tumble and

wrestle. Alistair comes out better and gets his arm round Colin's neck.

Gaaarrrggg! Lemme go! You're chokin' me.

ALISTAIR: Give me that knife then.

COLIN: Alright, alright, but you're gonna be responsible.

ALISTAIR: What are you on about?

COLIN: If I don't get the doctor to Luke, it'll be your fault.

ALISTAIR: Oh yeh? First it was the Queen, now it's the best doctor in the world dropping everything to go to Australia with you. Pull the other one.

COLIN: It's true. I'm meeting him today. Straight up.

ALISTAIR: The world's best doctor's meeting you?

COLIN: Today at noon. I met this bloke, see, who knows him. He's arranging it. Luke's gonna be cured. It's all set.

ALISTAIR: Honest?

COLIN: I told you, straight up.

ALISTAIR: Sodding brilliant. Just wait till you get back to Australia. You're going to be a blinking hero you are. [*He hands Colin the knife.*]

COLIN: Some hero with a broken neck.

ALISTAIR: Sorry. Hey, you will be back before, you know, before they, you know.

57

COLIN: No worries.

ALISTAIR: It's just that I hate cold baked beans.

COLIN: Yeh? Well I love 'em [*He leaves.*]

Ted is waiting. He looks a proper misery-guts. Colin enters and hands him a chocolate frog. Ted looks up and smiles.

TED: Hi digger.

COLIN: Is it all set?

TED: The doctor's meeting us here in a minute.

COLIN: He a quick packer?

TED: What?

COLIN: A quick packer. Or is he like Arnie Strachan's Mum, always making lists and losing them.

A woman in white coat walks towards them.

TED: Colin . . .

COLIN: Doesn't matter. He won't need much. And Dad can always lend him a couple of shirts – unless he's got a really fat neck.

TED: Colin, this is Doctor Graham.

She holds out her hand.

DOCTOR: Hello, Colin.

COLIN: [*shaking it*] G'day.

TED: Dr Graham is one of the most experienced cancer experts in the world.

COLIN: Great. When can you leave? They've got seats on all flights, including tonight.

DOCTOR: Colin, it's not that simple.

COLIN: You don't have to worry about getting a seat near the dunnies . . .

DOCTOR: I've been in touch with the hospital in Sydney where Luke is.

COLIN: Excellent. Dad always says: 'If you want a job done, go to the top ma—. . . er . . . woman.

DOCTOR: I rang early this morning and I talked to one of the doctors treating Luke. He's in good hands, Colin. They're the best in Luke's unit.

COLIN: Mum and Dad will want to pay you back for that call.

DOCTOR: The doctor explained to me exactly what type of cancer Luke has. His prognosis is correct. Luke can't be cured.

TED: Colin, I'm . . .

COLIN: BULL!

DOCTOR: He's going to die, Colin.

COLIN: BULL!

DOCTOR: The exact location and the advanced stage of
     the disease means Luke is one of the unlucky
     ones . . .

COLIN: BULL!

DOCTOR: It's very rare . . .

COLIN: [*running off, yelling*] Bull!

[*Ted calls after him and then runs after him, the doctor leaves.*]

*Colin enters Alistair's bedroom, completely wrung out and lies
down on his bed. Iris and Bob and Alistair hover outside the
room.*

BOB: He's just sort of lying there.

IRIS: It's delayed shock. Alistair, leave your scalp alone.

BOB: Had to happen sooner or later, poor kid. You heard
     your mother.

IRIS: I wonder if we should get the doctor in?

BOB: No, plenty of rest and he'll be right as rain.

IRIS: Let's leave him in peace then.

   *They tiptoe out. Alistair tiptoes back and sits beside
   Colin.*

ALISTAIR: Didn't it work out then?

COLIN: They tricked me.

ALISTAIR: Who tricked you?

COLIN: They reckon he can't be cured. He said he knew the best doctor in the world. I phoned Mum and everything.

ALISTAIR: I reckon you won't be going home a hero then.

COLIN: I can't go home now. Ever.

ALISTAIR: Great. I'll be a nervous wreck by the time we grow up.

COLIN: I can't face them. I promised I'd make it alright.

ALISTAIR: We're only kids. We're not supposed to make everything alright.

Pause.

I was reading this book about ancient tribes in the Amazon. Do you know, they never get things like heart disease and other, you know, things.

COLIN: Cancer?

ALISTAIR: It's an unknown disease up the Amazon, is that.

Colin sits up.

COLIN: Maybe they do get it, but they know how to cure it.

ALISTAIR: I shouldn't think so, not ancient tribes.

COLIN: Maybe while we've been using up all our technology on spaceships and computers and stuff they've been quietly discovering a cure for cancer. I've got to go there!

ALISTAIR: Do you know how much that would cost?!

COLIN: I've got my return ticket to Australia, I can have a stop-over.

ALISTAIR: Your plane won't be going past the Amazon.

COLIN: Well, I'll stow away on a cargo ship.

ALISTAIR: You're soft, you are.

COLIN: I'll go down the docks tomorrow and jump a cargo ship to South America.

ALISTAIR: But what about snake bites and cholera and cannibals and stuff?

COLIN: It'll be worth it to see Mum's face when I walk into that hospital with the cure.

ALISTAIR: You want locking up, you do.

COLIN: Tried that, remember?

ALISTAIR: Just don't tell me any more about it. Mum says she's never seen my dandruff so bad. I can't take the stress.

COLIN: I wonder what time high tide is?

Pause.

ALISTAIR: Colin . . .?

COLIN: Here we go. Alright, what problem have you thought of this time?

ALISTAIR: Well, like, you'll need someone to give you a leg up and help you hack through the jungle and stuff. I'd better come.

COLIN: OK.

ALISTAIR: When did you say we're leaving?

COLIN: Tomorrow, the quicker the better.

ALISTAIR: Good.

Pause.

I didn't think you were going to make it back in time today.

COLIN: Yeh, well I had things to do.

ALISTAIR: What, like?

COLIN: Reckon they're so smart. I fixed them.

ALISTAIR: What have you done this time?

Colin takes out his knife and demonstrates slashing tyres.

COLIN: Some of those fancy doctors are going to be late for their fancy dinners at their fancy houses cos they got no air in the tyres of their fancy cars any more.

ALISTAIR: Oh God.

COLIN: I slashed them to pieces. I would have done them all if Ted hadn't found me.

ALISTAIR: You know what you've done, don't you? You've gone and dropped him right in it.

COLIN: What are you rabbiting on about? I did it, he's alright.

ALISTAIR: It was him that took you there.

COLIN: [*realising*] I'd better go see if he's alright tomorrow.

ALISTAIR: I thought we were going to South America tomorrow?

COLIN: Next day, alright?

ALISTAIR: Alright.

At Ted's place. Ted is moving around with great difficulty. The doorbell rings.

TED: Who is it?

COLIN: [*from outside*] It's me, Colin Mudford.

TED: The key's under next door's mat.

COLIN: Next door's?

TED: You don't think I'm daft enough to leave it under

mine in a neighbourhood like this do you? Go and fetch it and let yourself in.

Ted struggles to a chair. By the time he has done so, Colin has entered.

COLIN: Oh no, Alistair was right. They bashed you up.

TED: You what?

COLIN: The doctors, they bashed you up cos of their tyres.

TED: The doctors didn't bash me up.

COLIN: They'll be looking for me then.

TED: No, actually they're looking for an Irish tow-truck driver with a red beard and a limp. I told them that's who I saw letting the air out of their tyres.

COLIN: Lucky for them I only let the air out instead of slashing them to bits.

TED: Lucky for you, you mean.

COLIN: Did you have an accident?

TED: Not exactly. Local hoons jumped me last night as I was leaving the hospital. Belted me round the head with a lump of wood and jumped up and down on me a bit. Hurt my foot.

COLIN: Why?

TED: I don't think they like me.

65

COLIN: Did you tell the police?

TED: They don't like me much either. Anyway, I didn't get a good look at them. [*He winces as he tries to move.*]

COLIN: I reckon you better go to bed.

TED: No can do. I've got to get to a phone somehow and let the hospital know I can't visit. Griff 'll be frantic when I don't turn up.

COLIN: I'll visit her for you – if you like.

Ted looks at Colin. He gets his wallet out and takes a photo from it and hands it to him.

TED: That's Griff.

COLIN: Oh.

Pause.

I'll visit him for you if you like.

TED: [*smiling*] Well, maybe if you just phone for me.

COLIN: Is that why they bashed you up, cos you and Griff are in love? [*Ted nods.*] I don't mind going to the hospital for you, honest.

TED: That's very good of you, but . . .

COLIN: No worries.

TED: Colin . . . Griff hasn't just got cancer. He's got AIDS.

COLIN: I read about that.

TED: I don't expect you want to go to the hospital any more.

COLIN: What time's visiting hours?

Pause.

TED: Give us your shoulder. I got a few things in the kitchen you can take to him for me.

In the hospital garden. Griff is wheeled in in a wheelchair. He is wearing a bright scarf over his head tied behind his neck. He is very frail.

NURSE: Well, think you've had enough fresh air?

GRIFF: Can I just sit out here a while?

NURSE: It's a bit chilly, love.

GRIFF: A few minutes, please.

NURSE: Just a few minutes.

The Nurse tucks a blanket round Griff's shoulders and leaves as Colin enters.

COLIN: Are you Griff Price?

GRIFF: Yes.

COLIN: I'm Colin, a friend of Ted's. He's a bit crook today. It's OK but, it's nothing serious. He wrote you this note.

67

Griff reads the note.

GRIFF: [*trying to be composed*] Did his doctor say how many days before he can walk?

COLIN: Don't think so. You don't look much like your picture.

GRIFF: I know. When I look in the mirror I give myself a fright.

COLIN: No, you look . . . um . . . [*He indicates the scarf*] . . . Nice.

GRIFF: The treatment made my hair fall out.

COLIN: [*embarrassed*] It . . . er . . . suits you.

GRIFF: Thank you, kind sir.

COLIN: Ted sent you this [*He gives Griff a brown paper bag, Griff opens it.*]

GRIFF: Tangerines! Oh, Colin, you're an angel!

COLIN: You like them?

GRIFF: Been craving for them, can't eat much any more. I always thought that when I saw my first angel it would have wings and a halo, not freckles and elastic-sided boots!

As Griff peels a tangerine, a Nurse strolls by with some-one in a wheelchair. The Nurse helps the patient up and they walk into the hospital leaving the wheelchair behind.

Want some? [*He holds out half a tangerine*] Or would
you rather peel your own?

COLIN: Thanks. [*He takes the half tangerine*] How long
have you and Ted known each other?

GRIFF: Six years. I met him in a sheet-metal factory in
Wales. We both had jobs there.

COLIN: Why did you leave?

GRIFF: Factory closed down last year. Spent months
looking for work. So we decided to try our luck in
the big smoke.

COLIN: How did you go?

GRIFF: A week after we got here I got sick. They did a
few tests and told me I'd got AIDS. I haven't been
too well since, so Ted took care of me till I had to
come in here. [*Griff rubs his finger gently over the
tattoo on his hand.*]

COLIN: I know what that means. It's Welsh for forever.

GRIFF: Forever.

COLIN: You'll be out of here soon. Prob'ly.

GRIFF: One way or another.

Pause.

It's very good of you to visit me. I appreciate it.

COLIN: It's alright.

GRIFF: Don't get many visitors.

COLIN: It's too far for your Mum and Dad to come every day?

GRIFF: They don't come.

COLIN: Not ever?

TED: I'm not their favourite person.

COLIN: Why?

GRIFF: Me and Ted, and . . . this. They can't accept things. [*He changes the subject*] Do you miss the Aussie sunshine?

COLIN: A bit.

GRIFF: When things got tough in Wales, we used to dream about emigrating to Australia; everybody here does. What do you do over there for a cheer-up?

COLIN: Um . . . We got Arnie Strachan.

GRIFF: Tell me about Arnie Strachan.

COLIN: He's got pet chooks.

GRIFF: Chooks?

COLIN: Chickens. He loves them chooks. Gave them all names. Hey, one day Doug Beal drove his trail bike into Arnie's Chook pen. Arnie was as mad as a cut snake – he got his Dad's sheep clippers and went round Doug's place and sheared his Mum's shagpile carpet!

70

GRIFF: Ow, don't make me laugh like that! It hurts!

COLIN: Sorry.

GRIFF: No, I like it. We don't get much to laugh at in here. What are you doing over here anyway?

COLIN: I'm . . . I'm on holiday.

The Nurse returns for Griff.

NURSE: Sorry, rest time, no more nattering.

GRIFF: Alright bossy. Will you come and see me again Colin? I'd like to get to know Arnie Strachan.

COLIN: Yeh, alright.

GRIFF: And tell Ted to hurry up and get better, eh?

COLIN: Don't worry. You'll be seeing him soon.

The Nurse leaves with Griff. Colin spies the empty wheelchair and puts his hand on it.

Sooner than you think!

Colin looks furtively around him then makes a run for it with the empty wheelchair.

In the hospital garden. Suddenly there are shrieks and laughter from out of sight. Colin races in pushing Griff in his wheelchair. Ted frantically pushes the wheels of the stolen wheelchair in an effort to catch up. They do wheelies and come to a halt, laughing.

GRIFF: I'm still faster than you are.

TED: I'm handicapped and you've got that Aussie racing goanna on your side.

The Nurse enters and looks at them frowning. Ted pulls a rug up under his chin and looks innocent. Colin and Griff also look angelic. The Nurse finds a spot some distance away and gets out her lunch.

GRIFF: You've worn me out.

TED: [*concerned*] Are you alright?

GRIFF: Never better. But no more what d'you call them? Wheelies?

TED: You know what you are, Colin? A genius.

COLIN: Could you put that in writing? I'll send it to Mr Blair at school.

GRIFF: [*tenderly, to Ted*] It's good to see you. I was worried.

COLIN: I reckon I'll just . . . um . . .

Colin leaves them and approaches the Nurse. Ted and Griff in the background talk earnestly and quietly.

G'day.

NURSE: Hello. You're getting to be a regular.

COLIN: I reckon.

NURSE: [*looking in Ted's direction*] Funny, I can't place that patient with Mr Price. Sure I've seen him before though.

COLIN: Ah, he's, ah, from another ward.

NURSE: Oh. Mr Price looks happy. I think you cheer him up. You know he's . . . quite sick.

COLIN: Yes.

NURSE: They all are in here.

COLIN: It's weird. Some of the people in here . . .

NURSE: What?

COLIN: I just noticed. Some of them don't look like they're going to die. I mean they look real crook and everything, but they don't look . . . miserable.

NURSE: Some cope better than others. I think it's the families that make all the difference. If they all rally round, I don't know, it seems to help.

COLIN: I reckon you're right.

NURSE: Oops, look at the time! I got to get back. Bye.

COLIN: See ya.

Ted beckons Colin over.

TED: Colin, I know you probably don't like soppy stuff. But we wanted to say thanks.

GRIFF: You'll probably never know how important this

little bit of time is to us, or how precious a gift you've given us.

TED: Now that was soppy!

They leave.

At Alistair's house. He is practising hacking through the jungle with the bread-knife. He has a colander on his head. Iris walks past.

IRIS: Nice game, love?

ALISTAIR: Er . . . yes Mum.

IRIS: Well, don't go wearing yourself out, pet.

She leaves. Colin walks past.

COLIN: What are you doing?

ALISTAIR: [*whispering*] I'm practising for the jungle. I made us a grappling iron out of coathangers to get on the cargo ship.

COLIN: Great.

ALISTAIR: Tomorrow, right?

COLIN: Well . . .

ALISTAIR: You said tomorrow a week ago! And three days ago! And yesterday!

COLIN: I've got to meet Ted tomorrow and help put that wheelchair back.

ALISTAIR: You're going to get caught, they're coming home early tomorrow.

COLIN: I'll be back in time. You should see how happy Griff is . . .

ALISTAIR: That's all very well, but the ancient tribes of the Amazon are probably giving their cure for cancer to some drug company who'll put it into pills and sell them for a million pounds. Each.

COLIN: It won't be much longer. Promise. Hey – Where's Wales?

ALISTAIR: Wales? WALES?!!

COLIN: Can you get the tube there?

ALISTAIR: It's another bloomin' country is Wales!

COLIN: Oh. Pity. There's some people there need a good talking to.

Colin leaves.

ALISTAIR: The two explorers hack through the jungle. Hack! Hack! The tsetse flies and the leeches and the heat drive them mad. Hack! Hack! And all the time the sound of the cannibals' drums gets louder and louder . . . Hack! Hack! Suddenly a cobra springs out of the undergrowth and sinks its fangs into the wimpy explorer's hand. Help! Help! He cries as he sinks to his knees in the quicksand. I'll save you! Says the tough explorer. He cuts into the flesh with his trusty blade and puts the wimpy explorer's hand to his lips and starts to suck out the poison . . .

*Alistair sucks his arm and spits and sucks noisily again.
Iris enters.*

IRIS: Alistair! What are you doing?

ALISTAIR: Er . . . Nothing . . .

IRIS: Get upstairs at once. I don't know what gets into
you.

Alistair goes. Iris watches him, worried.

Kissing his hand now! Maybe I should get him one of
those child psychiatrists. Bob! [*She goes.*]

*At the hospital. Ted wheels Griff on. Griff's head hangs, his eyes
are closed. His hand falls over the side of the wheelchair arm
rest. Ted stops and tenderly replaces it. A Nurse enters and feels
for Griff's pulse. Colin enters bearing a bag of tangerines. He
realises Griff has died and places the bag on Griff's lap. The
Nurse wheels Griff off.*

COLIN: I'm glad he wasn't alone.

TED: It wasn't enough. He asked for them.

COLIN: His family? [*Ted nods*]

COLIN: Couldn't you get them to come?

TED: No.

COLIN: Pikers.

TED: They'll come now, they'll take him back to Wales for
the funeral.

COLIN: They've got no right!

TED: It's alright, it's where he needs to be. Home, see?
     Colin, will you do me a favour?

COLIN: Sure.

TED: Stay with me a while?

COLIN: Sure.

•

*At Alistair's house. There are yowls from out of sight. Iris leads
Alistair in by the ear. She has the back door lock in her hand.*

IRIS: I'll give you sorry, my lad.

ALISTAIR: Ow ow ow ow ow ow!

IRIS: What else have you two been up to?

ALISTAIR: It wasn't me it was him!

IRIS: What have I told you about lies?

ALISTAIR: He said he'd torture me if I told.

IRIS: Nothing but trouble since he got here.

ALISTAIR: I tried to stop him, Mum – honest.

COLIN: Alistair! I'm back. [*He enters*] Oh-oh.

IRIS: I'm very, very disappointed in you Colin Mudford.
     We invited you over here to take your mind off . . .
     things and all you've done is lie to us and deceive us.

COLIN: Sorry.

IRIS: South America! Are you out of your mind? Do you
    know what the sun does to Alistair's rash?

COLIN: Sorry.

IRIS: Bit late for that now, after you've been gallivanting
    all over London with unsuitable types.

COLIN: I haven't . . .

IRIS: Don't try and deny it.

COLIN: They weren't unsuitable.

IRIS: How do we know that, when we haven't even had
    the pleasure of meeting them?

COLIN: Well, actually . . .

IRIS: I don't want to hear any more from you young
    man. Upstairs with you and it's cold baked beans
    for tea – for you both! And be grateful! [*She goes.*]

ALISTAIR: Sorry I blabbed, but I was being tortured . . .
    [*Colin looks at him contemptuously*] Well, actually,
    Mum told me keeping secrets would make my
    dandruff worse.

COLIN: Doesn't matter. If the ancient tribes had a cure for
    cancer, we'd have seen it on TV by now.

ALISTAIR: Prob'ly. You won't be able to see Ted any
    more.

COLIN: Oh yes I will.

ALISTAIR: [*Alistair covers his ears*] Don't tell me, I don't
want to know.

COLIN: I've invited him here to tea.

ALISTAIR: [*starts whistling*] I can't hear you. [*Whistles*]
I'm not listening.

COLIN: Tomorrow.

*Iris wheels a tea trolley in, Bob places some chairs around.
Alistair joins them and they sit formally. Alistair reaches for a
biscuit from the trolley, Iris slaps his hand. A kitch doorbell is
heard and they jump up in apprehension. Colin tears out of the
room in his usual bullet-fashion.*

COLIN: I'll get it! [*He returns with Ted*] Auntie Iris, Uncle
Bob, this is my mate, Ted. The one with his mouth
hangin' open is my cousin Alistair.

*Alistair shuts his mouth, there are 'pleased-to-meet-
yous' all round. Ted is sat down. They all look at each
other smiling stiffly and then all say something at once.*

IRIS: Cup of tea, Ted?

TED: Thank you. [*Iris starts to pour, Alistair grabs the
opportunity to take a biscuit*] Nice home you have.

IRIS: Thank you Ted. Bob's a bit of a do-it-yourself
enthusiast.

BOB: Only way. I'm not paying hundreds of pounds to
some cowboy to mess up my plumbing, eh?

TED: Quite right.

BOB: You into home improvements?

TED: Er, no, not much.

IRIS: The biggest hardware centre in Greater London's not far from here. Bob could show you round.

TED: Another time perhaps.

BOB: What do you do for a crust, Ted?

TED: I'm unemployed.

COLIN: He's not a dole-bludger, but. He had to stay home and look after Griff.

Ted looks like he is going to cry. His teacup starts to wobble. He puts it on the trolley.

IRIS: Top up, Ted? [*He shakes his head*] Biscuit? Piece of cake?

Suddenly Iris picks up a bowl from the trolley. She hands it round [missing Alistair] everybody takes a tangerine.

They're lovely, these. Take your mind off . . . things.

Ted begins to cry. Iris motions to Bob to take Alistair out of the room. He does so. There is silence as Ted cries. Colin is struggling not to cry too. Ted pulls himself together a little.

[*kindly*] Would you like your cup of tea now, love?

Ted tries to answer, but he cannot. Colin, his voice very shaky, answers for him.

COLIN: He'll be right, thanks.

TED: [*to Colin*] I think I'd better go. [*To Iris*] Thanks very much.

IRIS: You don't have to go, love. Stay until you feel better.

TED: No, I'll be alright now.

IRIS: Are you sure?

TED: Thank you, yes.

IRIS: Alright, take care of yourself then.

TED: Thanks.

IRIS: Bye then.

> *Colin sees Ted off. Iris studies the tangerines, puzzled. Colin re-enters. He stands looking at his aunty Iris. He starts to cry.*

COLIN: I want to go home.

IRIS: Oh pet.

> *Iris holds out her arms. Colin runs to her and cries in her arms loud and long. As he quietens, Bob and Alistair return.*

BOB: Alright, then?

IRIS: He's alright, aren't you love?

COLIN: Yeh.

IRIS: Bit homesick, that's all.

COLIN: It's not just that. I've got to go home.

IRIS: You will, love, when things are . . . you know.

COLIN: You don't understand. I have to go home and be with Luke.

IRIS: You can't love.

BOB: You don't really want to go back to all that, do you?

COLIN: Yes.

IRIS: No you don't.

ALISTAIR: Yes he does.

IRIS: Shut up Alistair.

COLIN: I got to go, auntie.

ALISTAIR: See.

BOB: You heard your mother, Alistair.

COLIN: Please.

ALISTAIR: Go on, let him.

Bob points out of the room and Alistair shuffles off. Bob gives him a hurry-up and follows.

COLIN: You can't stop me. I have to go home!

IRIS: Now listen to me, love, put it out of your mind, you can't go home. You'll understand when you're older that it's for the best.

COLIN: No! You're wrong!

IRIS: Now stop this nonsense.

COLIN: I told you, I'm going home!

IRIS: Listen to me Colin. I'm sorry things are so hard for you love, but you're not going to Australia, and that's that. And just in case you and Alistair have got any notions of cooking something up, don't waste your time. They won't let you on the plane without a guardian to sign the forms. Now, I don't want to hear another word about it. OK? OK??

COLIN: OK. I won't mention it again.

IRIS: There's a good lad.

At the airport. There is a small counter with a woman behind it. Ted paces up and down. Colin enters lugging his suitcase.

TED: I thought you weren't going to make it.

COLIN: Yeh, took me a while to figure out how to get the new lock off.

TED: Nobody woke up, then?

COLIN: Snoring their heads off.

TED: Better get checked in.

They go to the desk. The woman takes Colin's case and his ticket.

WOMAN: Travelling alone?

COLIN: Yes.

WOMAN: [*to Ted*] What relationship are you to the traveller?

COLIN: Mate.

TED: Friend.

WOMAN: Guardian?

COLIN: That's right.

WOMAN: Sign here please, so the young man can travel unaccompanied. [*Ted signs.*]

TED: [*they walk away from the desk*] Well, this is it then.

COLIN: I hope you don't get into trouble, signing and stuff.

TED: Nah. Besides, I'm used to trouble. Think about me sometimes . . . and Griff.

COLIN: I got you a present. Here. [*Colin digs in his pocket and hands Ted a pink scarf.*]

TED: Great! My favourite colour.

They hug. Ted puts the scarf on and flips it over his shoulder.

See ya Colin.

COLIN: See ya Ted.

Ted leaves.

Auntie Iris and Uncle Bob rush in. Alistair puffs up behind.

IRIS: STOP! Stop that boy!

COLIN: Shit!

Colin makes a run for it. They all try to grab him, including the airport woman, there is much tripping up and tangling [some of it done by Alistair who is on Colin's side]. Finally, they collar him.

WOMAN: Alright, now what is going on here?

IRIS: This young man is trying to leave the country illegally.

COLIN: No I'm not. I'm an Australian citizen, I got my passport and I'm going home!

IRIS: You're an under-age Australian citizen and you're not going anywhere!

WOMAN: Who exactly are you people?

BOB: I'm this boy's Uncle, he's under my care.

WOMAN: You're his guardian?

BOB: Legal guardian I am.

WOMAN: But what about the man who signed the form?

IRIS: Who signed? Colin, who was it? Was it your friend Ted? He's in big trouble my lad, big trouble.

WOMAN: I'd better get the airport police.

COLIN: No! The police don't like him, please don't.

BOB: That won't be necessary, thank you very much. There's no real harm done. We'll sort things out.

IRIS: Now then Colin, We're going to have no more . . .

COLIN: The plane'll be leaving in a minute. Let me go, please?

ALISTAIR: I think you should let him.

IRIS: Shut up Alistair.

ALISTAIR: No, really . . .

BOB: You heard your mother.

COLIN: I've got to go.

IRIS: I'm warning you Colin Mudford . . .

COLIN: I'm going. You can't watch me every minute of the day and night! If you lock me up I'll escape . . .

ALISTAIR: He will, you know.

BOB and IRIS: SHUT UP Alistair!

COLIN: I'll get home somehow.

BOB: Come on Colin lad, don't you think we've had enough of all this?

ALISTAIR: [*yelling*] Enough! I'll tell you who's had enough! I've had enough, that's who's had enough! [*Stunned silence*] I've got him thinking up all sorts of tricks to get me in trouble and you telling me what to do night and day. Do this Alistair, do that! Well I've had it! What makes you grown-ups so smart that you know what's best for everybody? You're not smart at all, any of you! He's the one that knows what's best for him and Luke, not you! He knows where he wants to be and he's goin' and that's final! [*Silence.*]

IRIS: Alistair . . .?

ALISTAIR: [*losing his bottle*] Sorry . . .

IRIS: Bob, our Alistair's growing up. Oh, Alistair.

BOB: Yes, well . . .

IRIS: Maybe the boy's got a point.

COLIN: Please . . .

IRIS: What do you think Bob?

There is a last boarding call announcement. Bob ponders.

BOB: Let the lad go home.

IRIS: I don't know what I'm going to say to your mother.

COLIN: Mum'll be right.

IRIS: Well . . . Be off with you then.

COLIN: I love you auntie Iris.

IRIS: Oh, stop that.

COLIN: Onya Alistair. Oh, here, I meant to give you this. [*He gives Alistair his Swiss army knife*] You might need it one day.

ALISTAIR: Aw, brill!

IRIS: Alistair, give that back. You'll cut yourself.

ALISTAIR: No I won't.

IRIS: Oh. Well be careful with it then. Look after yourself Colin, love.

ALISTAIR: [*getting a letter out*] I nearly forgot. The postman brought this for you. It's from Buckingham Palace.

Colin opens the letter and reads aloud.

COLIN: Dear Mr Mudford. Her Majesty's sympathies are with all who suffer through illness. May I, on her behalf, wish your brother a speedy recovery. Signed . . . I can't read the signature . . . Palace Li. .

ALISTAIR: [*he had read it*] Palace Liaison Officer – oops!

BOB: Her Majesty's sympathies! Huh!

COLIN: [*screwing the letter up and throwing it at Alistair and mimicking Bob*] Get me started on the Queen!

ALISTAIR: [*drop-kicking it back*] Ought to be stuffed and
    put in a museum!

BOB: Too right! Say hello to everyone for us Colin.

COLIN: Yeh, see ya. [*They kiss him.*]

ALISTAIR: See ya Colin.

They wave. Colin waves back.

ALISTAIR: [*to Bob*] They're charging by the minute in
    that car park . . . Eh Dad?

BOB: Right son.

*They hurry off toward the car park. The last call for
Colin's plane is heard.*

LOUDSPEAKER VOICE: Now boarding from gate number
    ten is Qantas flight number two to Sydney via
    Singapore and Melbourne. This is your last call, your
    last call for Qantas flight number two to Sydney via
    Singapore and Melbourne.

*The businessman from the flight over hurries on, he is
busy checking his ticket and does not notice Colin.*

COLIN: G'day! Fancy meeting you again!

The businessman looks at Colin in horror.

What number's your ticket? Let's have a look. Hey,
    you've got the seat next to me again. Where you
    goin'?

The businessman backs away, shaking his head. He turns and runs off, waving his ticket.

You'll miss the plane! Poor bugger must have indigestion again.

Colin heads for the plane.

Luke is in his hospital bed. Mum and Dad sit beside him. Colin enters. Luke sits up and flings his arms wide.

LUKE: Colin! Colin! Colin!

Mum and Dad look up. Their faces light up. Colin rushes into Luke's arms.

THE END